Library of Congress Cataloging-in-Publication Data
Gaiman, Neil.
    The day I swapped my dad for two goldfish / [Neil Gaiman and Dave McKean].
       p.   cm.
    Summary: After trading his father for two goldfish, a boy and his little sister go on a rollicking adventure around town to get him back.
    ISBN-10: 0-06-058701-6 (trade bdg.) — ISBN-13: 978-0-06-058701-7 (trade bdg.)
    ISBN-10: 0-06-058702-4 (lib. bdg.) — ISBN-13: 978-0-06-058702-4 (lib. bdg.)
    ISBN-10: 0-06-058703-2 (pbk.) — ISBN-13: 978-0-06-058703-1 (pbk.)
    [1. Brothers and sisters—Fiction. 2. Fathers—Fiction. 3. Barter—Fiction. 4. Humorous stories.] I. McKean, Dave, ill. II. Title.
PZ7.G1273 Day 2004   2003067683
[E]—dc22

Book design by Dave McKean @ Hourglass
❖ Revised edition 2004
09 10 11 12 13 SCP 10 9 8 7 6 5 4 3

The DAY I swapped

my DAD for TWO goldfish

HarperCollinsPublishers

Lost:

One book. If found, please return to Hayley Campbell
(although she may be too big for it)
or Maddy Gaiman (although it may be too big for her).
No fish, please.

Wanted:

One halibut, must be in good working order, own fins,
no skate please.
Will swap two infants, one called Yolanda, one called Liam.

Offers to Mr. David Tench McKean, Esq. c/o The Publisher.

One day my mom went out and left me at home with just my little sister and my dad.

My dad sat in front of the television, reading his newspaper. My dad doesn't pay much attention to anything, when he's reading his newspaper.

We went up to my bedroom.
My little sister tagged along.
I showed Nathan my old transformer
robots, and my baseball cards, and my books.
I showed him my old punching bag and
my penny whistle that Mommy said made
her head ache when I blew it. I showed
him my old spaceship that didn't float in
the bath anymore, and the puppet with
the tangled strings, and I even showed him
Clownie, my clown that I sleep with.

And every time I showed
him something, Nathan said,

No.

We went downstairs.

I thought for a bit.

Some people have great ideas maybe
once or twice in their life, and then
they discover electricity or fire or
outer space or something.
I mean, the kind of brilliant ideas
that change the whole world.

Some people never have
them at all.

When my mother came home I said, "Mom, can we buy some goldfish food?"

My mother looked at me sharply.

"Right," said my mother, and she picked up the bowl of goldfish and handed it to me. "You can take these goldfish over to Nathan this minute, and don't you come back without your father."

"I told you so," said my little sister.

"And you can go with him," said my mother. "Fancy allowing your brother to swap your father for two goldfish and a bowl. The very idea."

So we went to Nathan's house.
He only lives over the road.
I Knocked on the door.

Nathan's mother came out.

Is Nathan here? I asked.

"Where did you get those goldfish?" she asked me.

"They were a present to Nathan from his Aunt Violet."

"I swapped them," I said. "And now I have to swap them back again."

What's that supposed to mean?

I asked Nathan.

Follow me,

he said.

We went upstairs to Nathan's bedroom. It was even messier than my bedroom. Nathan had an electric guitar, a big white one.

I swapped this electric guitar with Vashti Singh,

he said.

Blinky had a very big house.
We went up to the front and rang the bell.

Blinky came down the big stairs.
He looked very pleased to see the
gorilla mask.

"Are you bringing
it back?" he asked.

"Yes we are,"
I told him.

Blinky made the butler give us ginger beer.

I liked it even though the bubbles tickled my nose.

My sister made a face.

"Now," I asked, when I finished the ginger beer, "where's my dad?"

"Ah," said Blinky. He went away again, around the side of the house.

I gave him the gorilla mask. He gave me Galveston
and a map he drew of how to get to Patti's house.

I'd never walked so far in my whole life.

While we walked, Galveston the Rabbit sat in my arms and made its nose go woffly. My sister tried to make her nose go as woffly as Galveston's, but she couldn't do it.

There was a little rabbit hutch there,
and next to the rabbit hutch was a little
run with chicken wire all around it.
My dad sat on the grass, in the chicken wire run,
reading his newspaper and eating a carrot.
He looked a bit lonely, and he had grass all
over his trousers.

Last week my little sister told everyone at school that I was adopted. The week before she told everyone at school that I was a space alien pretending to be me.

When we got home my mother said things like, "Just look at the state of him!" and she made him go and have a bath and she put all his clothes into the washing.

While Dad was in the bath, my mother told me off.

And when she'd finished telling me off she made me promise, cross my heart, that I would never — ever — swap my dad for anything ever ever again.

And I promised.

So I won't.

But I never promised anything
about my little sister. . . .

f i n

Afterword

This book started like this.

My son, who is called Michael or Mike these days, but was Mikey back then, was angry at me. I'd said one of those things that parents say, like "isn't it time you were in bed," and he had looked up at me, furious, and said, "I wish I didn't have a dad! I wish I had . . ." and then he stopped and thought, trying to think of what one could have instead of a father. Finally he said, "I wish I had goldfish!"

And he stomped off to bed.

I was awed by the idea. Of course one ought to be able to trade a father for goldfish. It seemed a very sensible thing to do.

I wrote the first sentence or two on my computer and then wasn't quite sure how it went after that, so I stopped and did other things.

A few years later I was in a hotel in Galveston, Texas, where I had gone to write a television script. I was stuck on the script, so I looked at the files on my computer to see if there was anything there that was interesting—and waiting for me was the first sentence of that book I'd started about the boy who swapped his dad for two goldfish.

I knew what the next sentence was, so I wrote it. And the one after that. Eventually I'd finished a whole book (and I'd named a rabbit Galveston), and wasn't much further along with my television script.

I gave the book to Dave McKean, who drew the magical pictures.

The boy and his sister are a little bit Mike and his sister Holly, who spent the first dozen years of their lives locked in a bitter and deadly cold war, and a little bit me and my sister Claire, who, oddly enough, did exactly the same thing through most of our childhoods, but actually rather like each other these days. But mostly they are just themselves.

I always wanted a really convincing gorilla mask.

Neil Gaiman
October 17, 2003